ANOTHER NIGHT AT THE MUSEUM

MILAN TRENC

Christy Ottaviano Books
Henry Holt and Company
NEW YORK

There's nothing better than a warm bath, Larry thought. He was soaking in the tub when he caught a glimpse of the clock.

"Oh my, I'm late for work!" He jumped out of the bathtub and into his blue uniform with shiny, brass buttons. You see, Larry was a night guard at the American Museum of Natural History.

"Late again, Daddy?" Melissa asked.

"Won't you eat supper?" Mother wanted to know.

"No time," Larry said. "The museum is waiting."

"Please, please, can I come with you?"
Melissa begged.

"It's bedtime, sweetie pie. Besides, you know
that night visitors are not allowed."

Larry arrived at the
museum just as the front
doors were being locked
for the night.

Inside, the chief guard was waiting. "I'll put you in charge of the Ocean Hall, my boy. I heard you had some trouble with the dinosaurs the other night."

The real story, as you probably know, is that Larry fell asleep and all of the museum came to life.

The Ocean Hall looked
harmless enough. Larry found
a chair and stretched out.

"Oh my!" Larry darted to close the windows. And what a sight to see! The Ocean Hall floor was submerged in water, and the giant octopus and blue whale had escaped.

"Come back!" Larry shouted after them.

Outside, the trees in Central Park were underwater.
Then Larry saw Melissa floating by on a mailbox.
"Melissa!" he shouted.
"I've come to save you, Daddy."

"How on earth did you get here?"
"I paddled, of course!" Larry helped Melissa scramble up to the roof.
"Did you leave the faucet running, Daddy?"

CREEAK!!!

Just then, the whole building shook violently.

The blue whale and the giant octopus had
dislodged the museum and were pushing it
down Central Park West!

The museum was sailing like a giant ship.
"Wa-hooo!" Melissa shouted as she used
one of the giant octopus's tentacles as a slide.

The marine exhibit creatures pushed the museum past the spires of St. Patrick's Cathedral. It missed the Empire State Building by an inch and almost knocked the Statue of Liberty's torch as it sailed toward the open ocean.

"Oh dear," Larry sighed.
The ocean was all around
him, as far as he could see.
"Melissa, where are you?"
he called.

But neither Melissa nor anybody else was anywhere to be seen.

"Excuse me, but maybe she is with the whale and the octopus?" a friendly orca suggested.

Larry held tight
to his trusty flashlight
and dove in.

Larry soon caught up with Melissa, who was busy swimming with the first amphibians.

Coelacanth, the living fossil fish, watched in disbelief. "Why is everybody coming back to the ocean?" she wanted to know. "Is dry land no fun anymore?" She looked at Melissa. "I remember when this dry-land craze started, some four hundred million years ago. . . ."

"Enough chatting!" Melissa heard her dad shout. "It's almost morning, and the museum will be opening soon. How in the world can I persuade the marine exhibits to take us back?"

"I'll help you, Daddy," Melissa assured him. "See, you have to ask them nicely, and"—she lowered her voice—"maybe you could offer them a reward, just this one time, of course."

Larry took Melissa's advice—and it worked
like magic! Soon the marine animals joined
forces to drag the museum back to its original
home on Central Park West.

"Please, slow down," Larry asked the blue whale as the museum floated near their apartment.

Through tightly shut windows they could see people sleeping peacefully in their beds.

And there was Mother, dreaming away, unaware of the chaos of the night.

"Let's fix this mess," Larry told Melissa as they swam through the open bathroom window. As soon as he turned off the faucet, the water level started falling rapidly. They hurried back out to catch up with the museum.

At last the museum was set in its usual place. There was just enough time to put everything back in order.

As the sun rose above Manhattan,
the museum was where it belonged, and
Larry and Melissa were heading home.

"Daddy, what did you promise
the animals as a reward?"
"I told them this was nothing
compared to the adventure I have
planned for tomorrow night!"

MELISSA'S FACTBOOK

Can a bathtub faucet flood Manhattan?

Not any time soon. An average faucet would take about one billion years to raise the sea level three to four feet. It would then take about eighty billion years to sink the Statue of Liberty up to its torch. In other words, if you left your faucet running at the time Earth was formed, by today the sea level around the world would have risen only 15 feet. A riverside building in Manhattan would be flooded only up to the second floor.

What is a living fossil?

A living fossil is an animal species that lived millions of years ago but didn't become extinct and still exists more or less unchanged. Such species include crocodiles, opossums, koala bears, and coelacanths (SEE–luh–kanths).

Is the coelacanth really 400 million years old?

Everybody thought coelacanths became extinct with the dinosaurs 65 million years ago. So people were very surprised when a living coelacanth was caught by an African fisherman in 1938. The coelacanth alive today is very similar to fish that lived 400 million years ago. An average modern coelacanth can live up to 100 years and grows to five feet long.

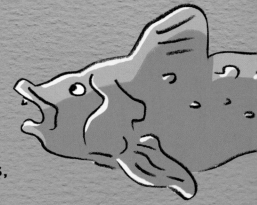

Could a blue whale and a giant octopus pull the Museum of Natural History?

The answer is a firm NO. While it is hard to estimate the weight of the Museum of Natural History, it is probably in excess of 200,000 tons. The blue whale, at some 200 tons of body weight, hardly stands a chance of pulling something a thousand times heavier. The giant octopus, as it appears in this book, is a product of the author's imagination, fun as it is. The largest documented specimen of octopus weighs less than 157 pounds (about 71 kilograms) and could hardly pull a doghouse let alone the museum. However, there is some scientific speculation that in the days of dinosaurs, much larger mollusks lived on the planet . . . but even they couldn't move the museum.

Will the next night at the museum be even crazier than this one?

Definitely yes.

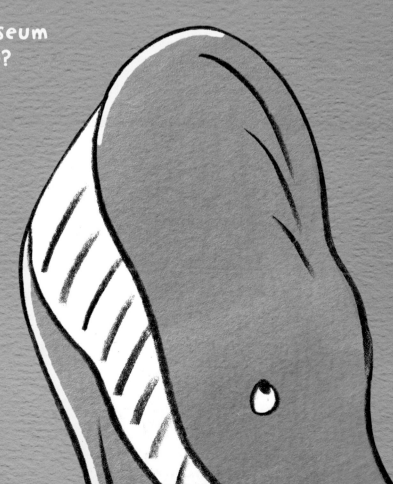

Henry Holt and Company, LLC
Publishers since 1866
175 Fifth Avenue
New York, New York 10010
mackids.com

Library of Congress Cataloging-in-Publication Data
Trenc, Milan.
Another night at the museum / Milan Trenc. — 1st ed.
p. cm.
"Christy Ottaviano Books."
Summary: When the night guard arrives at the Ocean room at the Museum
of Natural History, he wonders if he left the bathtub faucet on at home.
ISBN 978-0-8050-8948-6 (hc)
[1. Natural history museums—Fiction. 2. Museums—Fiction. 3. Floods—Fiction.
4. New York (N.Y.)—Fiction.] I. Title.
PZ7.T7194Ano 2013   [E]—dc23   2011043473

First Edition—2013
Pencil, Ecoline watercolors on Fabriano Artistico watercolor paper,
and Photoshop CS2 were used to create the illustrations for this book.

Printed in China by South China Printing Co. Ltd., Dongguan City, Guangdong Province

1 3 5 7 9 10 8 6 4 2